# The DADDIES BOAT

by
## Lucia Monfried

illustrated by
## Michele Chessare

A PUFFIN UNICORN

PUFFIN UNICORN BOOKS

Published by the Penguin Group
Penguin Books USA Inc., 375 Hudson Street, New York, New York 10014, U.S.A.
Penguin Books Ltd, 27 Wrights Lane, London W8 5TZ, England
Penguin Books Australia Ltd, Ringwood, Victoria, Australia
Penguin Books Canada Ltd, 10 Alcorn Avenue, Toronto, Ontario, Canada M4V 3B2
Penguin Books (N.Z.) Ltd, 182-190 Wairau Road, Auckland 10, New Zealand
Penguin Books Ltd, Registered Offices: Harmondsworth, Middlesex, England

Library of Congress number 89-25689
ISBN 0-14-054938-2

Published in the United States by Dutton Children's Books,
a division of Penguin Books USA Inc.
Designer: Barbara Powderly
Printed in Hong Kong by South China Printing Co.
First Puffin Unicorn Edition 1993
1 3 5 7 9 10 8 6 4 2

THE DADDIES BOAT is also available in hardcover
from Dutton Children's Books.

For my mother and daddy,
of course
L. M.

For my mother and father
M. C.

On Friday afternoons
in the summer,
the Daddies Boat
comes to the island where we have a beach house,
bringing mostly daddies for the weekend.

Mommy says it's a silly name,
but we call it the Daddies Boat anyway
because that's the way it's always been.

During the week
until the Daddies Boat comes,
there's just the two of us
and my cat,
who spends most of the time in the flower garden
when she's not chasing beetles.

It's okay with the two of us
but not just right
like it is when we are all together.

We have an outdoor shower
where you can look up and see the sky

and a raspberry bush just for picking,

and I never have to wear shoes

except in the store with the sign
that says NO BARE FEET

and at camp.

Every night, after my bedtime stories,
I go to sleep to the sound of the ocean.

And even though there's always the telephone,
I still can't wait
for Fridays, when the Daddies Boat comes.
I wake up early—
I can't help it—

and at camp I can't tell if the time goes fast or slow.

On the way home, we shop for a special dinner

and pick flowers to fill the house.
Instead of two places at the table
I set three.

We get the barbecue ready
and then it's time.

The dock is always crowded
with people just like us
waiting for the Daddies Boat
out on the water far away,

coming closer,

and I'm looking and looking—
and then finally
it's near enough for me to see

my mommy,

and I hug her
and she hugs me

and hugs Daddy

and then we go home.